THINGS THAT BURN

A. M. ROGERS

An imprint of Enslow Publishing
WEST **44** BOOKS™

Please visit our website, www.west44books.com. For a free color catalog of all our high-quality books, call toll free 1-800-398-2504.

Cataloging-in-Publication Data

Names: Rogers, A. M.
Title: Things that burn / A. M. Rogers.
Description: New York : West 44, 2023. |
Series: West 44 YA verse
Identifiers: ISBN 9781978596108 (pbk.) | ISBN 9781978596092 (library bound) | ISBN 9781978596115 (ebook)
Subjects: LCSH: American poetry--21st century. | Poetry, Modern--21st century. | English poetry.
Classification: LCC PS584.R644 2023 | DDC 811'.6--dc23

First Edition

Published in 2023 by
Enslow Publishing LLC
29 East 21st Street
New York, NY 10011

Copyright © 2023 Enslow Publishing LLC

Editor: Caitie McAneney
Designer: Tanya Dellaccio

Photo Credits: Cover (burning font) WSY imagens/Shutterstock.com; cover (hose) saravuth/Shutterstock.com.

All rights reserved. No part of this book may be reproduced in any form without permission in writing from the publisher, except by a reviewer.

Printed in the United States of America

CPSIA compliance information: Batch #CS23W44: For further information contact Enslow Publishing LLC, New York, New York at 1-800-398-2504.

*For everyone in blended families
trying to blend.*

AUDREY HEPBURN SAID,

Everything I learned I learned from the movies.

Audrey is my FAVORITE
actress, ever.
I have a poster
of her in my room.
I can't tell you
how many times
I've watched *Roman Holiday*.
It's a story about a princess
who runs away in Rome
for just one day.
The whole day
she does only the
things she wants
to do.

DECISIONS

By the end
of the movie,
she's returned
to her princess life.
It's full of boring duties
and responsibilities.
But it's *her* choice.

It sounds nice
to have a choice.

FEELING FREE

That's another one
of the reasons
I love acting
so much.
When I'm up
on stage,
I feel … free.

I get to *choose*
how to be.
When
you're
acting,
you're allowed
to feel
whatever
you want.
You're allowed
to be
just who
you want to be.
And I can be
just me:
Harper Williams.

MY FEELINGS ON STAGE

Heart,
pounding.
Blood,
rushing.
My
body
and
brain
working.

Theater can change the world.
I know it has the power
to change me.

But the question remains:
am I good enough
to change other people?

Lots
of chances
to act
in Los Angeles.

In this mid-sized California town?
Not so many.

THEY NEVER ASKED

I haven't seen
Mom
in person
since
Spring Break.
I live with Dad
since Mom
moved away.

Neither of them asked
where I wanted to be.
They never asked
if I agreed
with their plans—
for me.

It's not that
I *didn't* want
to live with Dad.
I just wanted
them to
give me
a voice,
give me
a choice.

WE TALK A LOT

But I miss Mom's
    smirk
    the smell of her perfume
    how she always knows how to cheer me up
    practicing lines together.

I miss her,
but I understand.
She had a good opportunity
in Atlanta.
And it's where
the rest of her
family lives.

She moved
early
this year.
I've yet
to spend
any real
time there.

AUDITIONS

Auditions
for our school play
Myths About Me
are coming up.

I could play the lead!
It's perfect.
Smart, with a lot of heart.

I've been practicing,
going over lines
every day.

There's this great monologue
where the protagonist
talks about trying to do the right thing.

Mom says she'll come see me
if I get the part.

So really,
it's got to happen.

And nothing
is going to get in my way.

WELL...

maybe one thing.

THE PROBLEM

I *can't* seem to get anything
done around my stepmom.

Learning lines
with her around
is *hard*.

I forgot to mention:
Dad and I live with her, too.

She's *everywhere*.
We moved into *her* house.

It's outside the town of Mountain Ridge.
That was after
last summer,
after the
wedding
(where I hardly knew *anyone*).

IT MIGHT SOUND FUNNY

But even my "room"
doesn't really feel like
mine.
It feels like a room
in my stepmom's house.

But this is my life,
and this is where
I live. So I guess
I've got to figure it out.

As Audrey said,
> *I believe in being strong when*
> *everything seems to be going wrong.*

MY STEPMOM

Ara works
at home.
She writes
screenplays.
I actually think that's
pretty cool.
(But I'd never
tell her that.)

Don't get me wrong:

She's nice.
But she's
always
in everything.

She's
always
cleaning or gardening or baking.
She's
always
asking
about my homework or, worse, my lines.

She says when
she's writing and
she hits a wall,
she's got to
move—
got to do *something*.

I just wish she'd do it somewhere else.

ARA

She's from Morocco.
She came here to study.
And maybe it was different there—
she talks of her large family,
and how they were
always together.
Loud
and proud
and
in one another's business.

Yeah, maybe it sounds *nice*,
but that's not *here*.
That can't be our life.

We met Ara in Los Angeles.
She goes there for work.
I guess she used to write
in the café where my dad
got lunch.

They met—
and I guess that was that.

TRYING

I'm always dropping hints
that I want her to back
off.
But she just doesn't get it.
I don't want
to spend
all this time
perfecting our lines.
We can never
be the *picture-perfect family*
they want
us to be.

What's worse:
Dad doesn't
get it,
either.

They're so busy making eyes at one another
that they don't even know when I'm upset.

DAD AND ME

We used to be
really close.
We used to spend
a lot of time
together
on hobbies,
like learning guitar
and shooting hoops.

Things change.

But still, I miss the days
it was just him and me.

He is very happy now—
they leave
little love notes
for each other
all over the house—
and I *want* that for him.

I just wish
he still had time left
for me.

DRAMA CLUB

Want to know
something about me?
This is the best part of my week.

When the teacher asks us
to imagine a flame,
I think of
fireflies I saw
in Georgia.

The other kids
imagine they
touch a candle
and
they're burned.

They place
charred fingertips
in wet mouths.

In my mind,
I sit with the fireflies
and try my hand
at creating light.

IT'S WARM

There's sweat rolling
in a long bead
down my back.

Early September and no sign of cooling down.
We get up to leave.

Someone cracks a stupid joke
about climate change—
Extended water-skiing season!

The teacher stops us,
          pokes holes in the humor.
The weather is getting strange, he says.

Dakota stands up.
      It's not just strange, they say.
      Things have got to change.

Teacher smiles—or does he?
      What are you going to do about
      climate change?

Dakota's eyes are hard.
      Speak truth to power
      and take action in
      every way we know how.
      Show them we
      mean business,
      and if they don't
      get it, they go.

DAKOTA

Dakota is possibly
the coolest person
at my school.
Can you imagine
saying something
like that
to a teacher?
They're so *sure*
of what's right.

When you see them,
this is the first thing you notice:

      Big afro.
Large glasses.
      Rainbow pin on their tee.

When you look deeper:
    I've never seen them
    be mean to another kid.
    They're passionate about social
    justice
    and the
    environment, too.
    They put their
    money where their
    mouth is.
    I know I've seen
    them at local protests,
    even if they're the only
    person carrying a sign
    in the street.

WHAT OTHER KIDS SAY:

Dakota's parents
are some sort of agents
that report for NGOs.

(I think that means they're
some kind of secret agents/
community organizers.)

Dakota moved here
from Northern California
after some tragedy.

Dakota was a child star
but doesn't like
to be recognized.

Yeah, it's a lot.
But Dakota's just *that cool*.

I don't know
about any of that stuff.

But
I've watched
them act,
and they're
really
good.

Besides,
some people
have a way
about them,
and Dakota does.

AFTER CLASS

Dakota is
surrounded by
a group of
their fans.
They smile
and joke
and easily make
new friends.

I have
a bit
more
trouble
than that,
and so I stand
awkwardly
again
in the back.

NEW KID

I'm not really
"the new kid"
anymore.

But sometimes
I think
that feeling
will
never
go away.

I've made some friends
at my new school
in Mountain Ridge.
Go Cougars!

Especially other kids
in drama club
like Nick and
Isabella and
Savannah.

We sometimes hang
after class.
But I still don't
really have
close friends.

No one I could tell my secrets to.

WHEN I LOOK UP

I'm surprised
it's almost
empty in front
of the building.
It's me
and Dakota,
and we're alone,
both of us
waiting for our rides.

Dakota
looks up
from their phone
and sees me.

I COULD

Two choices:
look away
and
go back
to scrolling.
Or

take a chance.

I don't know what it is
that pushes me
toward the latter.

*Do you really believe
what you said?
That people
can change
where the world's at?*

FAR AWAY

Dakota's eyes
fog over—
like glass
rubbed smooth
by salty ocean waves.

People are funny, they say. *Then again ...*
Even before Marsha P. Johnson
was at the Stonewall riots,
she was the
Saint of Christopher Street.

They throw their bag
over their shoulder
and shrug.

WHO'S MARSHA P. JOHNSON?

I ask.

Dakota doesn't make fun
of me for not knowing.
Another reason to like them.

*One of the
drag Queens
in New York City
who helped the LGBTQ community.*

That's cool.

*Sometimes it can take the world
a little while to catch up.
But there are people out there
doing good work.
All of us can do more
to make the world
a better place.*

I TAKE A BEAT

I don't know what to say.
Do more. Okay.
But what?

    Finally,
    Are you ready for auditions tomorrow?

Dakota smiles
and shrugs.
I could use some practice.
Do you want to go over lines tonight on
FaceTime?

    Seriously? I ask. *Yeah!*

We exchange numbers
and then their
mom pulls up.
I catch a flash
of her
short Afro
and golden hoop earrings.
She waves a hand
in our direction.

Dakota waves back
to her
and calls
back to me,

See you tonight, Harper.

HARPER!

Dad calls from the
window of his pickup truck.

I throw
my book bag *(thud)*
in back
and get in.

Hey, Sprout.

Dad looks like me:
All-American.
Clean cut, conventional, WASP-y.

On days he's not
on call,
he picks me up
from school.
We listen to
rock 'n' roll
and blues.
It's literally
the only
time it's just
the two
of us
anymore.

SHAKE UP

So I'm surprised when
Dad pulls into In-N-Out.

    Seriously? I ask.

What I don't say: Isn't Ara expecting us home?

He leans back
and gives me a smile.
Come on, he says,
My treat. Let's go wild.

This is the best
because it's been FOREVER
since it's been just Dad and me
doing anything.

Two vanilla shakes later,
and we're sitting in the booth.

I got you this, Dad says,
and he slides a book across
the table.
It's a book about Audrey Hepburn—
and I'm really touched.
It's about how she lived through World War II,
even helped the war effort.

This is SO cool.
And I mean it.
It makes me feel like
he's been listening to me.

THINGS ARE GOING GREAT ...

I'm so glad
Dad's not on duty
until tonight.
He's a firefighter
at the local station.

That means we don't have to hurry
because there's nowhere
he needs to be.

He works long shifts,
even sometimes
SLEEPING
at work. *(Ew.)*

But not tonight.
And right now,
it's just us two.

We laugh and joke.
I tell him all about
Drama Club.

Then Dad gives me a look,
and my heart sinks.

BRAIN FREEZE

So ...

    (So this *isn't* about
    spending time with me.)

Dad takes a breath,
then continues.

*You know you're going
to be a big sister soon.*

    Yeah, I forgot to mention that, too—
    Ara is eight months pregnant.
    A "picture-perfect" family.

I sit back in my seat
and stare
into my almost-empty
paper cup.

He doesn't pick up
that talking about this
is the last thing I want to do.

DAD'S TALK

He uses phrases like,

"We're a blended family"

and

"I know things are different"

as if I don't already know that.

But what really lights me up:

*I know Ara's not your mom—
but she's part of our family now.
She's part of your family, too.*

IS THAT ALL?

I ask.
And I glare.

Seriously.

I just want to enjoy my shake
without feeling like I need to throw up.

I suck on the end of the straw
so it makes a loud
sound
that doesn't invite more feedback.

YOU MIGHT THINK

I would be excited
to be a big sister.

I *am*.
But I'm
also
afraid.
Will
my
Dad
even
have
time
left
for
me?
Will
our
relationship
go
up
in
smoke?

Will I feel like even more of an outsider
in this picture-perfect family?

DAD STUDIES ME A LONG MOMENT

He's smart enough to see
this isn't going anywhere.

Yeah, he says finally.

No more
laughing
or
jokes
or
the
feeling
that
we're
doing
something
just
to
spend
time
together.

Let's go home, I say finally.
*I've got lines to study
and homework, too.
Besides,
I'm sure Ara's
wondering what we've been up to.*

STATIC, AND THEN NOT

The radio cuts through
our silence,
and the reporter
drones
on
and on.

It hasn't rained
for
weeks
and weeks.

It's important we don't
use the water
unless it's absolutely
necessary.

So when we get home,
Dad loads the dishwasher
but doesn't turn it on.

DAD SAID

endings

can just be the
beginnings
of new stories.

When he and Mom
split,
it seemed
like
an
ending.

Then he met
Ara and he saw
his new beginning.

But he didn't get
it wasn't a new beginning
for me.

BABY BUMP

Ara brings a tagine (a Moroccan dish)
to the table.
Dad dives in,
turmeric staining the corners
of his mouth yellow.
I push it around my plate.

> *How was your day, Harper?* Ara asks.

I shrug.

> *How's audition prep?* Dad asks.

I open my mouth
to tell him how excited
I am: the part
is perfect, and I'm
sure I'm going to nail it—

And then, *Ooof—*
Ara laughs,
puts a hand across her stomach.

> *Is she kicking?* Dad asks.
> He gets up and crosses the table
> and forgets I exist.

HARPER—

Do you want to learn how
to make maamoul?
I've had a craving for it
all day. Baby likes sweet, doesn't she?

I count the items on the counter:
      ghee
      olive oil
      flour
      sugar
      rose water
      date paste
      almonds

No, I say.

What happened to a good old chocolate cake?

Audrey said,
      Let's face it: a nice creamy chocolate
      cake does a lot for a lot of people.
      It does for me.

My mind returns to a recipe
for normal:
      Vinegar chips and baseball games.
      Mom, Dad, and me driving an hour
      for cherry picking.
      Sticky s'mores between my fingers.
      Old movies and pizza on Friday nights.
      Playing catch with Dad in the park.

All without Ara.

I WAIT

I keep checking
the time
and waiting
for Dakota to call.

And meanwhile,
I try to prep.
I say the lines
forward and backward
and
backward and forward.
But nothing
seems to stick.

Finally, I return
to my "room"
because
others in the house
are loud and baby-obsessed.

They're looking
through baby names,
trying on different
sounds for the person
she will be.

At first,
I kind of wanted to join in,
but I realize that
it's not meant to be.

LOOK AGAIN

I check
my phone
every few
minutes
to make
sure
I don't miss
Dakota.

I can't
miss
Dakota's
call.

IT RINGS

Mom.

Heyyyy, she says. *How's my budding star?*

I tell her
all about the part,
and then—

Hey, honey, can I talk to your dad for a sec?

I take the phone downstairs
where Dad and Ara are now watching TV.

    It's Mom, I say.

He sighs,
which is like
a punch
in the gut.
Since no matter what,
she's still *my* family.

And then he takes the phone.

It only takes half a minute for them
to start screaming at each other.

BAD RELATIONSHIPS

Some people
can get over bad relationships,
and some people can't.

My parents fall strongly in the second camp.

I'm not sad they split up—
both are better off apart.

But it'd be nice if they'd
get over their anger

and figure out how
to make a new start.

It'd be nice
if they could
do that
for me.

A RING

a circle of trust
heartfelt vows
a happy family

broken.

It didn't happen
all at once,
but slowly
day by day.
More fights.
Fewer date nights.
Then one day …
all that was left
were charred remains.

WAITING FOR THEM TO STOP FIGHTING ...

I grab an ice-cold glass of water
and go into the living room
to work on my lines.
I would go upstairs—
but I want my phone back.
When Mom called,
I forgot for a moment
about my call
with Dakota.

Now,
I can't help
but feel nervous.

Now,
I count
the seconds
on the dishwasher's
digital clock
in the other room.

I can't
miss the call.

THEY'RE STILL AT IT

I think
about going
in
and
saying
I'm expecting
a call.

I don't know
if that would
mean anything to them.

I sort of don't
want to step in the middle.

(I already *am* in the middle.)

But as
I work
up
the
nerve,
Ara
enters
the room.

A RING, REVISED

I didn't mean
for it to happen.
I wasn't thinking, and
I didn't plan it.
But there it is—
a circle of water
on wood—
on the heirloom
side table from
Ara's family
that she
brought from Morocco.
When she sees it,
she starts tearing up.

> *How many times,*
> she wants to know,
> *have I asked you to use a coaster?*
> *You know this table was made by my*
> *grandfather.*

IT'S NOT THAT I DON'T CARE—

I do—
but she didn't even bother
to listen
to my point of view.

I don't know what to say,
so I say nothing at all to her.

Instead I keep mumbling
my lines, over and over,
trying to become
anyone else.

*Maybe I can't do anything,
but that doesn't mean I can't try.*

*Maybe I can't do anything,
but that doesn't mean I can't try.*

*Maybe I can't do anything,
but that doesn't mean I can't try.*

ARA'S SHAKING

She's so mad.
And suddenly
I'm mad, too—
why should I have
to watch out for
her family heirloom?

Besides,
nothing in this house
is *mine*. No matter what,
I'm messing up *something*.

In the back of my mind,
I know that's not fair.
But right now,
I don't care.
Not while my parents
are fighting in the other room
and I've likely
missed
the call I could not miss.

Finally, Ara huffs
because I'm "not listening,"
and then she walks
out of the room.

SOBBING

I want to close the door
on fat, pregnant tears.
On hormones raging
and enemy lines drawn.

But even if I close the door
and even if I don't see it
or hear it,
it's still there.

So instead,
I slink back into
the living room,
empty now.
The TV plays
to no one.

*Maybe I can't do anything,
but that doesn't mean I can't try.*

HUNG UP

Hey, Sprout,

Dad says when
he comes to return my phone.
He looks uncomfortable—
like maybe he feels
bad for fighting with Mom
in front of me.
I flip the phone
and see I have three
missed FaceTime calls
and a text—
Hope everything's ok.
See you tomorrow in class.

ARA WAS PRETTY UPSET.

That's it. I can't hold it in.

> *Yeah, well.*
> *I'm upset, too,* I snap.

Harper—
    I recognize
    Dad's warning
    tone
    and
    I know
    I'm on
    thin ice.
    But my anger
    is white hot
    and I feel
        myself falling through.

WHY CAN'T WE GO BACK TO THE WAY THINGS USED TO BE?

*I don't want a new family.
I don't want
a new mother,
a baby sibling,
a new house,
or
a world falling down
around my ears.*

DAD'S ANGER

It's white hot.
The blood vessel
on his temple
is throbbing.
Wait a minute, now—
he starts,
but he's cut off.

CUT SHORT

Dad's work phone
starts to ring.

He *has* to answer it,
and so he digs
in the pocket of his jeans.

We're not done, Harper.
His normally calm voice
is sharp as a knife.

Then he answers the call.

Normally,
I might be afraid
of the consequences
of everything I just said
out loud—of how I really feel.

But
my attention
is grabbed
by what's
on the TV screen.

THE END OF THE WORLD

That's what it looks like.
I'm waiting for
a voiceover to prove
this is just part of
a trailer for some
new action movie.
But the newscaster says,

> *A wildfire has broken out*
> *in Terra Ridge, just west of the*
> *mountain range.*
> *Firefighters are rushing to put out*
> *the flames,*
> *which are spreading quickly.*
> *Right now winds are still,*
> *but the situation could change rapidly.*
> *We advise people*
> *to be ready.*

WHEN YOUR DAD'S A FIREFIGHTER

You sort of get used
to late nights.
You get used to missed
dinners
and quick out-the-door sights.

But you never get used
to the fear
that
they
won't
come
home.

Especially when they're going into something
that looks like THAT.

But,
on the other hand,
when your dad's a firefighter,
you know
the world is always
burning
somewhere.

Firefighters
are trained to
do what's right,
to be ready
for any fight.

And my dad is.

FAULT LINES

When Dad hangs up,
he looks around the room
like he forgot what
we were doing here.

But then his eyes
settle on me.
I stand my ground
because this was
NOT
all my fault.

I'd like you to apologize to Ara, he says.

      Not a chance, I think.

But I know
I shouldn't say *that.*

Instead,
I stomp upstairs to my "room."

HALF AN HOUR LATER

I'm still mad.
I still don't think
this was all my fault.
When Dad peeks in my door,
I'm turned away
and
pretending to sleep.

I hear the jingle of
his truck keys.

Good night, sweetheart, he says
               in a voice so
               that I *know* he thinks
               I'm asleep.

I think about
       turning my head
       getting up
       giving him a hug.

But
what if
he tells
me to
say I'm sorry
again?

Besides,
I'm still mad.

He's gone
before I get the chance to decide.

NO UPDATES

I keep my eyes
on the news
the next morning,
but there aren't
any updates.
So I guess
they're keeping
the wildfire
at bay?
Ara is not
downstairs
(and I'm kind of
relieved).
So I get
on the school bus
as if it's any other day.

That's when I realize
I totally forgot
about Dakota last night
and those missed calls.

DAKOTA'S OUT

I keep looking for them
because I want to
say sorry for being a no-show.

Then
I find out
they're not
in today.

I look like a total flake.

I ASK AROUND

If anyone knows
what's happening
on the other side
of the mountain.

A few classmates
live over there,
but none of them
seem to be in today.

I figure
school
would be canceled
if it were anything
too serious.

Even the auditions
are still on.

After last night,
I'm not prepared.

NOT GOOD

Auditions take place
in the last period of the day.
I'm so nervous
I can't focus.
I'm thinking
about my dad
and my mom
and Dakota
and all the rest.

My legs are shaking
and
there's too much energy.
I speak too loud.
I forget
my lines
at the halfway mark.

I blow it.

I can see the director
is unimpressed.
Maybe theater can change the world.
But it seems I can't.

SINKING

That feeling
when you know
something isn't
going to happen.
Also the feeling
before something
bad happens.
I know I won't
get the part.
That's pretty
obvious.
I just hope
that's the *only*
bad thing
that happens
today.

AFTER SCHOOL

It's the first time
I've seen Ara
since yesterday.

We haven't spoken
about what happened
last night.
I won't bring it up,
and I hope she won't either.

I want to call Dad,
but I know I can't.
If all goes to plan,
he'll check in
tonight,
like he always does.

THINGS THAT ARE DIFFERENT WHEN THERE'S A WILDFIRE

We used to open
the windows to the air.

We used to turn
the fans on so they would move
the air around the room.

We used to be
in bed with our faces to the moon,
the breeze crawling
under our noses like ants,
bringing picnic smells of flowers in bloom.

Right now,
the windows are closed
and the curtains are drawn
and the only sound
drones on and on
from the air purifier,
which hums and hums
like the cicadas used to do.

THE FIRE ACROSS THE MOUNTAIN

The idea of it looms,
but there's nothing much
about it on the news.
Instead,
they talk about gun violence
and a drawn-out court case.
They talk about the Pope
making a visit somewhere
and the drought that's
lasted more than 20 years.
Maybe it's my imagination then,
but I can feel the fire.
I can feel
the ground
shaking with fear.
There are no birds
flying in the air.
But if it were
really a threat,
we would already
be gone.
Wouldn't we?

DAD CALLS

It's right at nine o'clock.
The same time he always calls.
I let out a huge exhale, relieved.

I don't have time to talk,
he says.
*But I just wanted
to say good night
and I love you.*

Just the sound of his voice
is a giant relief.

What is it like?
I want to know.

He doesn't mince words:
*It's bad, Sprout. But we've got lots of firefighters.
I'll see you for breakfast, okay?*

The fact that he's planning to be home?
Another big relief.

ARA AND ME

We continue to move around
what happened last night.
I make my own dinner
before she has a chance
to make one for me.

Mac 'n' cheese.

And I clean up well
so she can't say anything else.

Then I go to my "room"
and try to think of
anything but my awful day.

I text Dakota.
Sorry I missed you yesterday.
Had some family drama at home.

I wait,
but there's no answer.

I'm pretty sure I've
screwed that up, too.

IN THE MORNING

My eyes feel like
dusty chalk.
I rub pebbles
of sleep away.

My skin is hot.
Leaving footprints
on the hardwood stairs
that disappear behind me.

My ears listen
for the sound of normal:
Dad in the kitchen—making eggs—
the news playing 24/7.

But there's a stone in my gut
because everything is still so silent.

MY VIEW FROM THE WINDOW

I don't see
the tire swing.
I don't see
the edge of the property.
I don't see
Ara's new flower bed.
I don't see
the sun.

It still looks like night.

I don't see these things

because

the world is covered in smoke.

WHERE'S DAD?

There's smoke in Ara's eyes, too,
when she appears behind me.

Her mouth holds
a worried expression.

> *He hasn't called,* she says.
> *The news reported that*
> *the winds have picked up—*
> *the very worst thing that*
> *can happen during a fire*
> *this size.*

MINUTES LATER

The radio
says
the wind
could go in
any direction.

*We don't
have a
handle on
this yet.*

The radio
says
danger.
It continues with words like
evacuation
and
find protection.

DECISIONS

I pull up a map
on my phone
with the information
they have so far.
The fire is on
the other side
of the mountain still.

I think we should stay here, I say.

Maybe this doesn't
feel like my home,
but
I can't imagine not being
here when
Dad gets back.

ARA HAS OTHER IDEAS

I think we have to go.

Ara starts putting random
things in a duffel bag—
a small photo album,
bags of spices,
a bottle of blue dish soap.

I don't think she
even knows what she's doing.

Look—
I try to show
her the map,
but she shakes her head.
Her mind is made up.

It's too dangerous.
You need to pack a bag.

I STARE, WIDE-MOUTHED

She pulls a hand
through her tangled hair.
Harper, I'm not messing around.
We're leaving in ten minutes.
Go pack a bag.

The radio is still running,
but I can't hear what they're saying.

You're not my mom, I say.
I'm shaking with rage.
I don't have to listen
to you.

        She's mad.
        I'm the adult here,
        and you'll do what I say.

I want to throw a fit.
I want to storm away.
But in a way, I know she's right.
And I'm afraid to disobey
because, really, I don't know what to do.

MY ROOM

For some reason,
the idea of leaving
this house
bothers me.

Yeah,
it's not *my* house,
but where else would we go?
Besides,
we cannot
get separated from Dad.

I go in my room.

First, I try to call Dad,
but there's not even
a dial sound.

Then I try to call Mom,
and there's no
dial sound either.

I have NO bars.
What is going on?

AUDREY HEPBURN STARES AT ME

behind
large sunglasses
from the poster
on the back
of my door.

What would you do?

But
there's no
answer from her.

PACK A BAG FOR THE END OF THE WORLD

What do you bring
if you might not come back?

Long sleeves,
heavy shoes,
long pants?

The internet says
to have
a face mask.
It blocks fire ash.

Water bottle,
flashlight,
first aid kit.

Is there room enough
for my memories?
Can I fold these things up
in the bottom of my bag
along with all the necessities?

I'm walking out the door—
sure I'll be back and this is just
a test—
when I spot the book
from Dad on Audrey Hepburn.
I shove it in
with the rest.

LEAVING THE ROOM

I find Ara
standing like a ghost
in front of the baby's room.

Together,
Dad and Ara
plotted and planned
to create
the perfect nursery.

You really *want to leave?*
    I ask.
    I hope
    she'll
    change her mind.

    Let's go,
    she says, really fast.

SILENCE

on the way to the evacuation site,
and for a long moment I hate Ara.
I know it's stupid.
She's just doing what
she thinks is best.
But I can't help thinking
that all of this is her fault.

After all,
we wouldn't even be here
if it wasn't for her.
We wouldn't be
evacuating
and Dad wouldn't
be missing.

Worst of all,
when he gets home,
he'll think *we're* missing.

UP AHEAD

It looks like the sun
is hanging on the edge
of the horizon.
It takes me a moment
to realize it's no sun,
but a wall of flame instead.
The fire is so big
and so fast
that it feels like
it's chasing us.
We're in a line of cars—
bumper to bumper
in a dangerous gridlock—
and there's so much smoke
we can hardly see the lights
in front of us.
Ara's knuckles are white
on the steering wheel,
and I feel like I'm
going to throw up.

We should've stayed home,
I say.

Ara doesn't say
anything back.

FLASHING LIGHTS

The only vehicles heading back
have light bars that flash
again and again.

These are police cars,
ambulances,
and fire trucks.

I wonder if Dad
is in one of them,
and I hope he isn't.

CHAOS

The bushes
and trees around us
catch on fire,
and deadly sparks
race along the blacktop.
My heart is in
my throat,
and there's blood
rushing in my ears.
To our left,
I see cars on fire
and people fighting
to free themselves
from seatbelts.

NOWHERE TO GO

There's nowhere to go.
We couldn't go back,
even if we wanted.

There's nowhere to go.

I hear myself,
reciting the first thing
from my brain:
the monologue
I memorized
for my audition.

*Maybe I can't do anything,
but that doesn't mean I can't try.*

There's nowhere to go.

I repeat the words,
in a way a kind of prayer,
again and again.

*Maybe I can't do anything,
but that doesn't mean I can't try.*

There's nowhere to go.

HOT

Ara's right hand
finds the back of my neck,
and she holds on to me.
There are tears
streaming down her cheeks,
and she is also saying something,
but I don't understand
what.
Her other hand
is resting on her stomach.

That's when I realize
we're going to die here.

MIRACLE

Suddenly, a truck with a snowplow
(it's not even winter)
pushes through,
and it moves other
burning vehicles aside.
I don't know who that guy is—
but he's just saved our lives.
The truck creates a small tunnel—
just what we need to get through.
Ara slams the clutch
and feeds the gas,
and
all of a sudden
we are out
and driving away, fast.

SHOCK

We move away from the fire
as quickly as we can.
The farther away we drive,
the lighter the sky gets.
Ara is silent,
but I'm still saying those lines—
over and over and over again.

> *You're in shock,* Ara says.
> *Try to breathe.*

If I'm in shock,
I wonder if she's in shock, too.
But she seems totally in control
while my heart is beating faster and faster
in my chest.
It sounds like rushing water
in my ears.

> *Can you try to put your seat back?*

Too late—
I can feel myself
falling forward in my chair,
the seatbelt jerking me
just as

everything
goes
black.

DARKNESS

buzzing in my ears

hot

voices

smell of rubber—

something tight on my chest

feels like floating

don't want to wake up

want my dad

BACK AGAIN

When I come to,
I see Ara's face.
She's unbuckling my seatbelt.
She's getting me to sip
hot, bottled water.
She's cupping the back
of my head in her hands
and smoothing my
hair back.

Behind her, there's a police car
and men in dark blue suits.
I look for Dad,
but I don't see him here.

>*How are you feeling?* she asks.

I want to say
>*awful*

but the word doesn't move past my lips.

I want to say
>*don't touch me*

but I don't have the strength.

I want to say
>*hold me*

but an EMT pushes in, and Ara moves back.

VITALS

Heart
screaming
in
my
chest.

Surely
his stethoscope
can
hear
it
pleading,

Is
my
dad
in
there?

DIAGNOSIS

The EMT
has pleasant
bedside manner.
He jokes while
making me
drink some
more bottled water
and counting
my heartbeats
between each breath.

But then
he talks to Ara
like I'm not
even there.

*She's okay.
It was a panic
attack. She just
needs to rest.*

Then,
to his partner:

*We've got another
load of people
coming in.
Just as before—
take the worst first.*

THEY HAVE A LOT TO DO, CLEARLY

They tell us
we're free to go.
But where?
Ara hears someone
talking about
a makeshift shelter
miles away
on the other
side of town.

> *We'll go there,*
> *she says,*
> *and get our bearings.*

I WANT MY DAD

but I know there's nothing to do.
We couldn't go back—
even if we wanted to.
I just have to hope
that he's alright.
I check my cell—
not a bar in sight.

IT'S LIKE A MOVIE OR A VIDEO GAME

The shelter
reminds me
of the aftermath
of a zombie infection.

It's fallout shelter
meets campground,
and there are people
pulling their
little belongings
out of singed cars.

There are also people
inside the building,
where they're handing
out supplies.

STAY HERE

Ara says.
*I'm going to
find the person
in charge.*

And I want to laugh
because she thinks
this is something that
somebody planned.

Why does
she think
she can
control everything?

I'M SURPRISED

A familiar face
hands me a bottle of water.

>*I'm glad you're here,*
>Dakota says.
>*And that you made it out okay.*

The liquid
slip slip slips
down through
the smoke
closing my throat.

>*You are okay … ?*

NOT EVEN CLOSE

I know I look a mess—
my face is smeared
with ash. I feel
singed
outside
and
in.

If I had water
left in my body,
I would cry.

Maybe that would
put out the fires.

B-RATE PERFORMANCE

I don't hide
my feelings well.
The acting definitely
won't sell.
I nod,
stumbling away.

HEY.

And suddenly
Dakota is next to me,
wrapping an arm
around my shoulders.
Holding me up.

    Do you want to talk about it? they ask.

And then
I'm spilling my guts.

We're sitting together,
backs against the wall.

I tell them everything—
Dad, the fire,
the fight,
not being able
to get ahold of Mom.
I tell them
about why
I missed their call.
Then my venom turns
on Ara.

She's the reason
we're in this mess.
I looked at the map—
the fire's nowhere near our home.
She panicked and then we left.
We almost died.

DAKOTA SAYS,

*That's a hard spot to be in.
Sometimes it's hard enough
listening to your mom or dad.*

It's the first
time I feel like I've
been really listened to
in a long time.

I feel like a weight
has been lifted.

Clearly,
I needed
to get it all
off my chest.

HOW LONG HAVE YOU BEEN HERE?

I ask.

> *Since yesterday,* Dakota says.
> *My mom already had an*
> *emergency kit ready to go.*
> *There was*
> *a wildfire up north*
> *a few years ago.*

Wow.

It's not exactly
a response that's
"best writing" material,
but I can't imagine
living through something
like this twice.
No wonder they
weren't at school
yesterday. They probably
left right away.
Dakota's voice is
thick and scratchy
like coffee grounds.

> *This is hard.*
> *I had so many nightmares*
> *after last time.*
> *I keep expecting*
> *to wake up.*

We talk for a while,
and for a moment
things almost feel okay.

AN ALMOST COMFORTABLE SILENCE

*Whenever you need to talk,
I'm here for you*, I say.

They push themselves up
and lift their
thumb up.

>*Thanks*, they say.
>*Better get back to it.*

ALONE AGAIN

I take out my phone
but there are still no bars.

Someone tells me—
The cell towers went down.

A few minutes later,
Ara shows up, and
she's holding her
phone like it weighs
300 pounds.

> *Do you have anything?* Ara asks.

No.

I BURN WITH RAGE

*This wouldn't have happened
if we had stayed home.*

I don't know why I say it—
only I want her to understand
the way I'm feeling.

I watch emotions
twist on her face,
and I know the words
have hit their mark.

She could say ANYTHING,
but this is what she says:

> *You should probably
> eat something.*

Then she's digging in her bag.

There's food under
the useless stuff.

She hands me
a granola bar.

I'm not hungry,
but I eat.

It's sandpaper
going down.

PAINS

Ara rubs
the small of her back,
her fingers moving
in small, firm circles.
She says,
I think I'll lie down.

She brought
two sleeping packs
with us.

She lays them out
on the rock-hard ground.

I lie down and zip it up
around myself.

I'm still hot,
but I don't
want her to see me.

TIME

I have no idea
how many hours
have passed.
We left the house
in the morning—
but everything
is still black.
It could be
already tomorrow
or even
another day,
and I would
have no idea.

SOME PEOPLE SLEEP

When I try,
there are nightmares.

I dream
I am surrounded.
I dream
I am swallowed.
I dream
about a wall of flames.
I dream
no one can reach me.

Instead of panicking,
I repeat those lines:

*Maybe I can't do anything,
but that doesn't mean I can't try.*

*Maybe I can't do anything,
but that doesn't mean I can't try.*

*Maybe I can't do anything,
but that doesn't mean I can't try.*

OUTSIDE

We're not supposed to be
outside
because
of
air quality.
But inside
I can't see
if there's a
wall of fire
coming for me.

There are
no
stars
or
moon.

Only the blackness
of a choked night.

Alone

I hold my cell phone
high,
looking
for
any
bars.
But the lines
are flat.
I compose
a text message
to Mom anyway
and hit send—
NOT SENT
remains
in angry red.

A NEW DAY

I wake up
with my book
in my face.

Audrey Hepburn is
smiling at me.

Ara is already awake.
She's looking through the album
of photographs she stuffed in her bag.

When she notices I'm looking, she smiles
a little, but sadly.

> *I want the baby to know her aunts
> and uncles
> even though they're far away.
> Want to see?*

I peer over her shoulder
at people who look like she does—
dark, thick hair
and wide-set eyes
and big smiles.

> *I miss them*, she says.

I START TO FEEL BAD FOR THINGS I'VE SAID

Ara wipes
a tear from
her eye.

I don't know
what to say.

If I reached out
to touch her,
would it be weird?

The moment passes
and everything
is weird anyway.

WINCE

I see her pull
a face.

Are you okay? I ask.

She pushes air
through her teeth
and then straightens
and smiles
at me.

It doesn't
look real.

> *Yeah*, she says,
> although I'm sure
> she's lying.

SHE STANDS

*We should see
if anything has happened,*
Ara says.

She tucks
the photos
in her bag
and wobbles away.

JUST 43 PERCENT CONTAINED

That's not enough.
The wildfire could
still make sudden
shifts, move in
directions
no one imagines.

We're told
not to panic
and
not to leave.

We wait another hour.
And one turns into three.

CHOKED

I stand outside again
because
I feel suffocated
inside.
It doesn't
make sense—
I know that.
If a wildfire's
coming,
it's better
to be
sheltered
and safe.

But I want to
know
when it's coming
and
I want to
know
what I'm facing.

COME INSIDE, HARPER

Ara coughs.

> *You shouldn't*
> *be out here*
> *where it's so hard*
> *to breathe.*

SELECTIVE HEARING

I want
to stay
outside.
I want
to run
home,
where
Dad will
be waiting
for me. So
I ignore her.

ARA CLICKS HER TONGUE

I groan,
but

finally

I do what
she says
and go in.

AS SOON AS THEY SAY WE CAN

we need to go home.
I wait an entire day
by the emergency radio,
waiting for what
folks on the ground
have to say.

We live on granola bars
and the bottles of warm water
volunteers hand out.

Dakota sits with me
at night.
Their mom and dad
wave from across the room.
We talk
about
everything
and
nothing—
music and news
and the books
we like.

They finger through
the Audrey Hepburn book
and read a few lines.

You can borrow it when I'm done, I offer.

NOW 87 PERCENT CONTAINED

I can
live
with
those
odds.

I can
already
see
Dad
stepping
off
the
porch.

I can
already
taste
the
blueberry
pancakes
he'll make.

Where have you been? he'll ask.
I've been a little bit worried.

WHEN I GET BACK TO ARA

people are already packing up.
Cars are already
pulling out of the lot.

We can go!
My voice
flies free,
and I'm already
grabbing
my things,
totally ready
to flee.

       Wait,
       Ara says.

Her eyebrows
are scrunched
together like
she's working
out a problem.

What is she waiting for? I think.
She doesn't get that we're free.

I say it again—
Let's go home. They said we can leave.

I push out the door
and into the parking lot.

Ara follows me.

HESITATION

*I have a bad feeling—
I don't know.
I don't think we should leave.*

I want to go home, I stress.
*Dad will be there.
He won't be able to guess
where we've gone.
We have to go find him.*

    NO, Ara says,
    stopping me dead in my tracks.

You just want to control everything,
I scream.
But you're not going to control me.

HURT

pools
in her
eyes,
and
I can't
stop.

You're not *my family!*

WATER

She's about to say something
but her eyes go wide
and she makes a sound
like a wild animal.
She looks down,
and my eyes follow—
there's liquid on the ground.
>*Oh*—
>she says,
>her mouth
>an O.

WHAT'S WRONG?

I regret
everything I just said
and did.

I wish I could
take it all back.

Are you okay?

I take a step
forward
and
she steps back.
I almost take
it personally,
and then I
realize
she's unsteady
on her feet.

THE BABY IS COMING

Too early.

I'M SCRAMBLING—

Are there any doctors here?
Ara is falling
to the ground now,
hands cut by
small rocks
in the parking lot.
She's breathing
in short gasps—
and it sounds
wrong.
Are you going to faint?
I ask,
and she doesn't
answer. She just
keeps breathing
like a clogged air vent.
I support her
as best as I can.

And I'm looking around for any help.

FACES IN THE CROWD

I recognize two—
Dakota and their mom.

I'm panting when they
reach me because I'm trying to hold
Ara upright.

She's *not*
doing well.

Dakota's mom
doesn't wait for
me to explain
before she takes the reins.

I'll bring the car around,
she says.
And we'll go to the hospital.
It's not far from here.
You guys stay right here.

Dakota takes
Ara's other side,
and we make sure she doesn't fall over.

ARA PASSES OUT

almost as soon
as we get her in the car.
I'm freaking out.
I try to call Dad.
I try to call Mom.
There's no
getting through.

THE HOSPITAL

I'm surprised to see
there are
a lot of people
waiting to be seen.
A little girl
is taken to
the Burn Unit
ahead of us,
and I want to be sick.
The nurses get
Ara a wheelchair,
but we have to wait
because they're so busy.

I find myself
again repeating those lines:

*Maybe I can't do anything,
but that doesn't mean I can't try.*

STRAIGHT BACK

When the nurses
wheel Ara away,
I'm left
in the hall
fighting back
tears of exhaustion,
frustration,
and guilt.

Are any of you next of kin?
The nurse asks.
I stare
because I don't
know what to say.

DAKOTA'S MOM ANSWERS FOR ME

She's her bonus kid.

*I've never heard
anyone say that
about a stepchild.*

*And her daddy's
a hero,
a firefighter
in that mess.*

It gives me a bit of courage.
I tell Dakota,
You don't have to stay.

You're crazy,
Dakota says.
*We're not going
anywhere.*

Tears cling
to my eyelids.

*Maybe I can't do anything,
but that doesn't mean I can't try.*

THE HALLS

are full of activity—
people being carted here
and there.
The wildfire has
created a giant mess,
and we're right
in the middle of it.
After half an hour,
Dakota's mom stands up.
I'm going to go get a coffee
from the cafeteria. You two want anything?

DAKOTA FINALLY BREAKS THE SILENCE

I'm sorry this is happening,
they say.

What about you? I ask.
I can't believe
you're here
with me
when you don't even
know what's happening at home.

My dad's
going to check it out,
but it's even farther
away from the fire
than we are now.
But you know,
it's just four walls
and a roof.
I know
the people
are safe.

I'm glad
because
I don't think
I could do that
again.

THE ONLY THING I CAN ASK

Do you want to talk about it?

THE STORY

Dakota stands
and starts to
walk the tiles
of the floor
like they're on
some kind of
tightrope.
Head down,
spine bent
like a great tree
weighed down.

> *We lost Granddaddy*
> *when the fires*
> *burned up north.*
> *He didn't want to leave*
> *his home. He said,*
> This is the home my grandfather built.
> *And it was a big deal, you know?*
> *It was the first home in his family*
> *that anybody* really *owned.*
> *He said,*
> *I'll see you when it's over.*
> *I was pretty young,*
> *but it rips my mom up sometimes.*

ANOTHER PAUSE

*We like to think
we've built our
skyscrapers and homes
away from nature,
where bad things
can't touch us.
But every part
of human civilization
is still part of this,
our troubled planet.*

THEY'RE RIGHT

The fire is
everywhere—
I see it
in ripped
clothing,
in charred
expressions,
in haunted eyes.

AND THEN
I REALIZE
SOMETHING

Sometimes
the only comfort you
can give is your presence.

You can't always make things
better,
but you can bear witness
to what's happened.

FINALLY—

after what feels
like hours and hours,
a doctor comes out,
her expression somewhat sour.

*Your stepmom has gone
into premature labor.
We're going to have
to do an emergency C-section.
They'll be taking her
back soon.
Sit tight.
We'll let you know
what's happening.*

HAVE YOU NOTICED?

Waiting is always the worst part?

FIDGETING

My fingers are moving
a mile a minute,
threading each other.
Over
and
under.
Under
and
over.
The only
reason I stop
is that Dakota
slips their
hand in mine
and squeezes.

I hear the sound
of Dakota's mom's shoes
along with someone else's.

Hey—isn't that—?

NOT A STRANGER

I have to rub
my eyes.
Still in the bottoms
of his firefighter suit.
Dakota's mom
must've seen him,
must've recognized him.
She must've told him
where we were.

Dad!

LINES

He looks me
over for something
wrong.

The creases in
his dirty face
of dried sweat
look like canyons.

And there are
rivers of tears.

HOW DID YOU FIND US?

Dakota's mom answers:
*I saw him coming in
and grabbed him.*

He says:
*Sprout,
I'm so glad you're safe.*

I DON'T WANT TO SHARE WHAT'S NEXT

*I've got something to tell you.
Ara's gone into preterm labor.
We were fighting—
I wanted to go home—
It's probably my fault—*

I can't get any more words out.

A HUG

He holds me tight,
and I let the tears
fall down my face.
Nothing's okay,
but at least
he's here.

I GUESS THIS IS GOODBYE

Now that Dad's here,
Dakota and their mom are going
to check on their
own future.

Thank you, I say.
For so many things.

    I'll talk to you soon, Dakota says.

Yeah, I say.
This time I promise I'll answer.

After they leave,
Dad and I go to the desk
to ask for news.

    The doctor should be out soon.

THE DOCTOR'S COMING OUT

I look
for signs
about
what she'll
say next.

> *Are you Dad?* she asks.
> Then:
> *Good news.*
> *You have a brand-new daughter.*
> *Your wife is out,*
> *and she's doing well.*
> *Do you want to see her?*

I can't help
the smile
that breaks
across my
face.

Dad and I
talk at
the same
time.
Yes!

REAL LIFE

None
of this
is
what I
thought
it would
be.

In movies,
women always
look so happy.

Ara
is already
sitting
up in bed,
but the baby
is not in
the room.

Too small—
she's in
the NICU.

ARA SOBS

and Dad
goes to her.

Everything's going to be okay,
I hear him say
over her tears.

As soon as they let me,
I want to go and be with her.
Ara says.

THOUGHTS FROM AN ORANGE PLASTIC CHAIR IN THE HALLWAY

I can't help but wonder
how much of what
Dad said is true.
Everything's going to be okay?
We've just lived
through one of the hardest days
I hope any of us will ever
have to go through.
Yet the way ahead
is equally unsure.

To tell you the truth,
I'm a little afraid
to meet my sister.
I can't promise
her a future
that's better
than today.
What do I tell her
about the
world she'll
get from us?

It's on fire.

NO MORE TIME TO THINK

Do you want to meet your little sister?

Dad stands before me.
And here it is.
I get up
on shaky legs
and follow
him through
the big doors
into a room
that hums,
full of
mechanical
machines.
When I enter,
there is a TON
of hand sanitizer.

THERE SHE IS

Her skin
is tinged blue,
and there's
a crown of
flaky skin
around her eyes.
She's dressed
in tiny everything:
      hat
      pajamas
      socks

Why doesn't she look at me?

      Don't worry, Dad says.
      For her, this is all new.

           Do you want to hold her?
           her nurse asks.

WHEN SHE SETTLES

My little sis
snuggles into
my arms,
and
I feel something
break inside.
The darkness
I felt
at the state of
the world
is pushed back,
at least a little bit.
I have this
overwhelming feeling
that
all is not lost.

WHAT'S IN A NAME?

What are you going to call her?
I ask.

> Dad smiles.
> *We haven't
> decided on that.
> We wanted to get
> your opinion.
> Maybe ... Audrey.*

My mouth falls open.
Ara's okay with that?

> *It was her idea.*

AUDREY HAS TO STAY IN THE NICU

But they have
a family hospital room.
Mom and baby are doing fine.

Dad turns on the TV
and we watch
for a while.

The nurses
come
in and out
and
out and in.

Dad tries to show me how
to change a diaper—
but I tell him
there's no way I'm doing that.

He laughs.

DAD GETS UP FOR COFFEE

I feel
Ara's eyes
on me.

>*I'm sorry.*

I'm surprised
because
I opened
my mouth
to say it,
but Ara spoke first.

So I respond:
I'm sorry, too.
I didn't mean what I said.

WE DON'T SAY MORE

It's funny:
I don't think we have to.

THE NEWS

comes late that evening:
the wildfire is over 97 percent contained.
That means
it's safe
for everyone
to return home.
If they have a home
to return to.

THE PLAN

Dad
and
I
will
go
and
see
what's
happened.
Then we'll
figure out
what
to
do
from
there.

JOURNEYS

We take a cab to the fire station
to get Dad's truck.
Then we drive
in silence.
My heart is
full of dread,
especially when
we start
to see
all the damage.

THE FOREST

It's little more
than charred
remains.
A few stubs
of leftover
tree trunks
stick out
of the ground
like skeleton bones.
My heart
is in my throat
by the time
we reach the
road that
turns toward home.
At first,
I think
we're not
in the right
spot.

WHAT'S LEFT

Burned foundation
crooked steel
and tile
and water pipes
that lead nowhere.

Our house
is no longer
a house.
It's just …

gone.

I think about
Audrey's room—
soft gray
with giraffes.
Everything
beautiful.
Now ash.

What are we going to do?

WE DIG

Looking for
anything.
Dad's expression
is hard to read.
It's like he's
a machine.
No emotion.
No reaction.
I try to
think of
something
to say
or some
kind of action.

WE LOAD THE TRUCK

With the little we find—
and
in the car
Dad pulls out his cell.
There's still
no reception.

> *We're going to have to call the*
> *insurance company,*
> *he says.*
> *We're going to have to figure out*
> *where we will stay*
> *and what we'll do next.*

RETURNING

When Dad tells Ara
at the hospital,
she takes a deep
breath and holds it.
I count the seconds
before she lets it out.
I worry about the table
her grandfather made.

It's all gone.

Finally, she says,
At least we're all safe.

When I see
Audrey,
I know she's right.

We're all
just lucky
to be here,
alive.

DAD SIGHS

I can't imagine
the thoughts
on his mind.

Let me make some calls.

Dad walks into the hall.
I'm looking out the window:
there is still green
from trees outside.
But there's hardly any light.
The smoke in the air
is hard to see through.

       Ara says:
       It's going to be alright.

And then Audrey
screams.

A FEW HOURS LATER

Dad has found us a place to stay.
The Happy Motel.
Yep,
that's the name.

It's one
room
for the four of us.

Ara and Audrey
will be in the hospital
at least a few more days.

Dad and I
will stay there
at night.

But during the day,
there's so much to do.

I FORM A PLAN

Something
small,
but it's
still something
I can do.

I see a thrift store
around the corner.

I find:
> a mini-crib
> a baby blanket
> a stuffed kangaroo

By the time I'm done decorating,
it looks …
well, not really like new.

I mean, it's a motel.

But it's a start.

ALL OUR PROBLEMS

They're
not
solved.

You may think
that a life-and-death
situation
would make it easier to
live together.

It doesn't.

Ara is still in my way,
and our behavior
is much the same.

But there's
a sense of ease, too.

Bad things happen,
but there's good, too.

WHEN I FINALLY GET THROUGH TO MOM

She's in tears.
I've been trying to call you,
she says.
*Do you want
to come stay with me?*

I think about it
for only a moment.
But I'm okay.
More than that,
there's A LOT of work still to do.

I need to find
a way
to prevent
this from happening
to anyone else
anytime soon.

I WANT TO KNOW

how Dakota and their family made out.

FaceTime,
no answer.

I type in the chat box:
I hope you're alright.

        Finally—
        All good. Talk soon.

I DO SOMETHING NEW

It starts
as a journal
and morphs
into a play:
a one-woman
show
about
my experiences
that day.

The words
rush out
so fast.

I let Ara read it,
and she says
it's really good.

She even says
she knows
a theater
that might
put it on.

THAT'S INSANE

It's also
really great
to make
art from
something
that made
me so
afraid.

I'm thinking
it'll be a benefit—
proceeds can
go to people
who've lost their homes.

Ara emails her contacts—
and it's a go.

BACK TO SCHOOL

It's weird
how everything resumes.

There ARE some new rules—
For example,
we can't spend
a lot of time outside
since air quality
is still so bad.
No sports.
No recess.
But thankfully
drama club is ON.

Nick, Isabella, Savannah, and I talk it out.
I look for
Dakota,
but they're not around.

People are already talking
about Dakota—
the rumors abound.

I FIND OUT

I didn't get the part.

Not a surprise.

Actually,
Savannah got it—
and I'm happy for her.

Besides,
I'm super busy
with my own play.

Everything is happening
so fast.

OTHER THINGS I'M REALIZING

There is no
picture-perfect
family.

We're imperfect,
and so is everyone else.

We
fight
and
get on
each other's
nerves.

(Especially with a baby
in a small motel room.)

HERE'S ANOTHER THING

We may not ALL
be
related
by blood,
but there are
a lot of things
that
hold us together.

We care
about the future.

In a way,
that makes
us all
part of a family.

MY SHOW

Only thing
now
is to
see it
through
to
the
end.

I know
my part
like
the back
of my
hand.

Just got to
spread the word.

I'M OUT

hanging posters
for my show
when I see a familiar face—

Dakota!
Where have you been?

They
saunter
up the
sidewalk
like they
haven't been
AWOL
for two weeks.

HOLD UP

>*Sorry,*
>Dakota grins.
>*I've been really busy.*

I ask
how
everything
worked
out.

>Dakota smiles.
>*Oh, fine.*
>*I need you to*
>*check*
>*this*
>*out.*

They hold up
a piece of paper.

DAKOTA'S MISSION

They found out—
it was on the news—
that a power company
was responsible.

Apparently their equipment
was 40 YEARS too old.

A spark from
the converter
lit up the brush,
which hadn't been
cleared in over a year.

LITERALLY
their fault.

I'm so angry
I see red.

DAKOTA SAYS

There *is* some good news:

> *The power company*
> *is settling for $12 billion.*
> *We're trying*
> *to use some of that money*
> *to turn the land*
> *into a nature preserve—*
> *one that will be carefully*
> *burned every few years.*
> *That way fires like this*
> *won't happen again.*

They go on:
> *Will you add your name?*

OF COURSE

The sight of my name
on a line under
thousands of other names
makes my heart glad.

But Dakota
doesn't seem satisfied.

> None of this feels like enough—
> they say.

Hey,
and I quote Audrey Hepburn for them—

*If you ever need a helping hand,
it's at the end of your arm.
Remember, you have another hand.
The first is to help yourself.
The second is to help others.*

Then, I joke:
*So I guess you and your parents
really are secret community-organizing agents?*

They laugh.

DAKOTA LOOKS AT MY FLYER

*This is cool,
Dakota says.
Nice work.*

*Want a free ticket?
There's a front-row
spot just for you.*

*Dakota smiles.
I wouldn't miss it for the world.*

WANT TO GO TO IN-N-OUT?

I ask.

>Dakota laughs.
>*I'm a vegetarian.*

*You know they
have a not-so-secret veg menu, right?
You like fries or grilled cheese?*

>Dakota grins.
>*OK.*

DAD AND ARA PICK US UP

and drop us off.

Thanks, Dad,
I say.

No problem,
he says.

I introduce
Dakota to Audrey,
who's buckled
in her car seat
in the back.

AN INSTANT HIT

Dakota makes a face
at Audrey,
who stares
in wonder.

I'm amazed
by her focus
and how
she looks
at the world.

I think
I could
learn
a
thing
or
two
from my
sister.

PROUD

I'm proud of you, Sprout.

Dad says it
when we're getting out
of the car at
In-N-Out.

He doesn't have to say
why.

I turn back
to smile.

Love you!
I shout.

IT'S NOT UNTIL
I SAY IT

that I realize
I'm talking to
all three of them.

My family—
Dad
Audrey
and even
Ara, too.

MAYBE

our family
isn't picture perfect.

Maybe the smoke
from our old fires
will always
hang around.

But here's
one thing I know—

I'd choose them
every time.

WANT TO KEEP READING?

If you liked this book, check out another book from West 44 Books:

EVERYTHING IT TAKES BY SANDI VAN

ISBN: 9781978595545

MY CALLING

The loudspeaker calls us down:

> *All juniors and seniors*
> *report to the cafeteria*
> *for the college fair.*

We follow
like cattle.

Mooing in groups
large and small.

Chewing gum
and checking phones.

Not me.

I'm ready for this.

Questions neatly written
on the last page
of my English notebook.

I'm ready
to leave this town
in my dust.

MY TOWN

feels like a leash
pulled tight.

    Whenever
        I   try
           to   wander.

TOO SMART FOR MY PANTS

Mom tells me
my brain is too big
for my britches.

Which is an
odd way
of saying

I'm too smart
for my pants.

Mom rolled her eyes
at my response,

when I told her:
it's breeches,
not britches.

In the original saying
anyway.

I looked it up.

See?

I'm too smart
for this town.

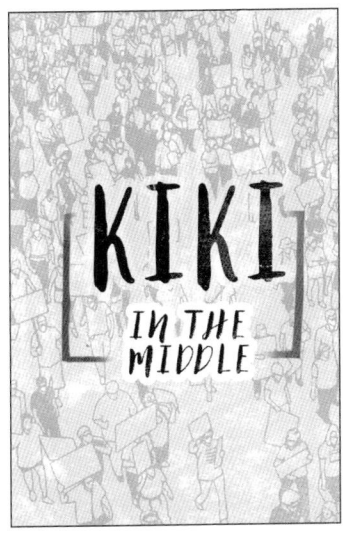

CHECK OUT MORE BOOKS AT:
www.west44books.com

An imprint of Enslow Publishing

WEST 44 BOOKS™

About the Author

A. M. Rogers is a writer and actress who lives on the shores of Lake Erie. She is passionate about creating community through storytelling and literature, and she believes we need to do something yesterday about climate change. She loves libraries and cats—and (you guessed it) library cats.